Frisky Falls Overboard

Written by
Catherine Shaw

Illustrated by
Steve Goodwin

Hello everyone, my name is Colin. I live in a small fishing village called Tideswell.

I work as a Coastguard with my dog Rocky. I have to make sure that people are safe when they are at sea, on the cliffs or on the beach.

If anyone is in trouble I can contact my friends who are always ready to help.

Now read how
Frisky Falls Overboard

It was a blustery morning and the sea was choppy.

Colin the Coastguard and his dog Rocky were looking out across Tideswell Bay.

In the distance they could see the ferryboat coming from Pebble Island.

The ferryboat was bringing the children from the island to Tideswell School.

The wind was blowing salty spray on to the children's faces.

The children were wearing life jackets and had their school bags with them.

Misha was sitting beside her friend Matt.

Suddenly, Misha noticed that Matt's bag seemed to be wriggling!

From the top of the bag a small furry head popped out.

A shiny black nose, a pink tongue and two brown eyes looked up.

"It's a puppy!" she gasped.

Misha laughed as the puppy squeezed out of Matt's bag and jumped on to his lap.

"This is Frisky, my new puppy," said Matt.

The other children saw what was happening and began to shout, "Woof!"

WOOF! WOOF! WOOF!

Suddenly, the ferryboat hit a huge wave. Frisky was startled and jumped on to the side of the boat but his paws slipped on the wet rail.

Over the side and into the
water he tumbled!

SPLOSH!

Matt yelled out
"Frisky!"

Frisky was being washed away from the boat.

Then something happened to make things worse!

SPLATT- SPLURR- SPLOTT!

The engine spluttered and stopped.

Some old plastic bags had wound around the boat's propeller.

9

Colin the Coastguard was in his office when the phone rang.

It was the ferryman asking for help.

This was an emergency!

What could Colin do?

Colin called Winch the tugboat captain.

He told him that the ferryboat needed help.

"Right!" said Winch, "I'll be there as fast as I can!"

Then Colin phoned Chesil the helicopter pilot.

He asked her to rescue Frisky.

"I'm on my way!" said Chesil.

Winch steered towards the ferry as quickly as he could.

He could see the children and the ferryman waving to attract his attention.

Winch carefully moved his tugboat alongside the ferry.

He threw a rope to the ferryman who tied it to the front of the boat.

As Winch towed the ferry to Tideswell Harbour, he phoned Colin, to let him know the children were safe!

But what about Frisky?

Meanwhile, Frisky was beginning to feel tired.

He was being swept further out to sea.

Slippy the seagull was flying high in the sky.

He saw that Frisky was in trouble and circled above, so that Chesil could see where to fly the helicopter.

14

Chesil flew the helicopter towards Slippy and spotted Frisky in the sea.

She lowered a basket until it was touching the water.

Chesil called out, "Don't worry Frisky, you'll soon be safe!"

When the basket was close to Frisky, he scrambled in.

16

Chesil made sure
that Frisky was
safely in the basket.

Then she gently pulled it
up into the helicopter.

Chesil radioed Colin to say
Frisky was safe!

17

Chesil flew the helicopter back to Tideswell.

By this time, Colin and Rocky were there with Matt and Misha to welcome Frisky.

As Chesil took off to return to base they all shouted, "Thank you!" and gave her a big wave.

They were so happy that Frisky was safe.

Next day, Colin went to Matt and Misha's school to talk to the children about what had happened.

The children realised how important it was to follow the rules.

That evening, Matt sent a letter to Colin, to thank him for helping to rescue Frisky.

Colin was delighted when he read the letter.

"That's kind of Matt," said Colin.

Rocky barked and wagged his tail.

Colin smiled, "Yes Rocky," he said, "we've found some new friends!"

THE END

Your Search Mission!

A. How many seagulls can you see on page 3?

B. How many life jackets can you see on page 4?

C. What is the name of the island where the children live?

D. What was wound around the boat's propeller?

E. How many flags can you see behind Colin on page 10?

F. What numbers are on the 'SEASIDE SAFETY' poster?

G. How many chimneys can you see (look very carefully!) on page 19?

H. What is the name of the ferryboat?

I. How many Colin badges can you count on page 20?

J. How many pictures of the helicopter can you see in the whole book (including the cover)?

Answers: A = 3 B = 8 C = Pebble Island D = Plastic Bags E = 4 F = 999 G = 8 H = Marlin I = 3 J = 8

Some of Colin's friends who are always ready to help:

Goodwin – Lifeboat Coxswain

Chesil – Search and Rescue Helicopter Pilot

Winch – Tugboat Captain

Embers – Fire Truck Officer